W9-BCX-834

For Max – K.B.
For Alyson, Martin, Poppy,
and Eden – K.L.

LONDON, NEW YORK, SYDNEY, DELHI, PARIS,
MUNICH, and JOHANNESBURG

First American Edition, 2001

Published in the United States by
DK Publishing, Inc.
95 Madison Avenue
New York, New York 10016

01 02 03 04 05 10 9 8 7 6 5 4 3 2 1

Library of Congress Cataloging-in-Publication Data
Banks, Kate, 1960 -
Mama's little baby / by Kate Banks ; illustrated by Karin Littlewood. - 1st American ed.
p. cm.
Summary: A mother shares lessons and love with her baby.
ISBN 0-7894-7904-4
[I. Mother and child - Fiction. 2. Babies - Fiction.] I Littlewood, Karin, ill. II. Title. I
PZ7. B22594 Mam 2001   [E] - dc21   2001028500

Color reproduction by Dot Gradations, UK. Printed and bound in Italy by L.E.G.O.

See our complete
catalog at
www.dk.com

Mama's Little Baby

Kate Banks

Illustrated by Karin Littlewood

DK Publishing, Inc.

Little Baby looks at Mama.
Outside a tree bends in the breeze.
Mama parts her lips and blows gently in Baby's face.
"This is the wind, Little Baby," she says.

Mama hands Baby a rattle.
Baby shakes it.
"Listen," says Mama.
She taps softly on the wooden floor.
"This is the rain, Little Baby," she says.

Baby coos loudly.
He clucks his tongue.
Mama clucks back.
"You're a little chick,"
she says.

A whistle sounds.
"That is a train,
Little Baby," says Mama.
"Where is it going?"
Baby kicks his legs
and waves his arms.
"Where are you going,
Little Baby?" asks Mama.

Mama pulls the covers over Baby's head.
Baby laughs.
"This is night, Little Baby," says Mama.
She pulls back the covers.
"And this is day," she says.

Baby cries. Mama lifts him up.
She turns him in a circle, around and around.
"You are turning like the world, Little Baby,"
she says.

Mama sits Baby on her lap.
She bounces him up and down.
"You're a little rabbit," she says.
And Baby laughs.

Mama turns on a lamp.
Baby looks at the shapes
on the wall.
"Those are shadows,"
says Mama.

Mama covers her eyes with her hands.
"Where is Mama?" she says.
Baby grabs Mama's fingers and squeezes tight.
"Here I am," says Mama.

Now Baby is hungry. Mama feeds him.
Then she rocks him back and forth.
Baby opens his mouth wide and yawns.
"You're a little lion," says Mama.

Baby is tired.
Mama lays him in his crib.
She whispers, "Sshhh, sshhh ...
That is the sound of the river."
And Baby sleeps.

When Baby wakes, Mama picks him up.
She hugs him close.
Baby smiles and touches Mama's face.
"You're my little baby," says Mama.